Katie La...

Room 14

Mrs. Dao

P9-CCM-764

"Growing Up Happy"

ETHAN HAS TOO MUCH ENERGY

An Emotional Literacy Book

Written by
Lawrence E. Shapiro, Ph.D.
Illustrated by
Steve Harpster

Ethan Has Too Much Energy
Copyright 2005, Courage to Change, LLC

All rights reserved under international and Pan-American
Copyright Conventions. Unless otherwise noted, no part of this
book may be reproduced, stored in a retrieval system,
transmitted in any form or by any means, electronic,
mechanical photocopying, recoding or otherwise, without
express written permission from the publisher, except for brief
quotations or critical reviews.

Author: Lawrence E. Shapiro, Ph.D.
Illustrator: Steve Harpster

Printed in China

Summary: This book tells the story of an active impulsive boy,
who with the help of a counselor, learns to calm himself down,
focus on one task at a time, and organize his work.

ISBN 0-9747789-4-X

Published by:
CTC Publishing
A Division of Courage to Change
10400 Eaton Place, Suite 140
Fairfax, Virginia 22030
1-800-942-0962
Fax: 1-703-383-3076
Web Site: www.couragetochange.com

For special discounts on volume orders, please call 703-383-3075.

Dear Boys and Girls,

Do you have lots of energy? Do you like to jump on the bed and do somersaults in the living room? Do you like to run around and play sports and swim and ride your bike? It's great to have a lot of energy, but some children have too much energy at the wrong times, and it gets them into trouble at home and at school.

Kids who have too much energy may have a hard time sitting still. They may have a hard time doing one thing at a time. They are often in such a rush to do things fast that they don't do them very well.

Children like Ethan, the boy in this book, need help in learning self-control. When children learn self-control, they can slow down when they need to and concentrate when they need to. When children learn self-control, they are better at listening to adults, and they don't get into trouble nearly so often.

Some children have too much energy all of the time. They don't do well in school, even though they are smart. Adults are always punishing them for misbehavior, even when they are trying to behave well. After testing by a doctor, we sometimes find out that these children have something called ADHD—Attention Deficit Hyperactivity Disorder. Maybe you have ADHD, or maybe you know other children with ADHD. Children with ADHD sometimes need a lot of extra help, and may even take medication to help them learn self-control.

If you are like Ethan and you need to learn self-control, this book can help. Even if you are not exactly like Ethan, you may need to learn better self-control and this book can help. Every adult will tell you that learning self-control is an important part of growing up, and it is certainly something to think about and talk about.

Your Friend,
Dr. Larry

Ethan jumped over an enormous cavern, trying to get away from the purple and yellow spiders. His feet just barely made it to the edge of the cliff, but he grabbed onto a long vine and swung himself to safety.

"Wait a second," Ethan said to himself, "this isn't a vine. It's a man eating snake!" And in a split second, Ethan was rolling on the ground, looking for a rock to conk that snake on the head.

"Ethan!" his mother yelled up from the kitchen. "It's time to get up!"

Ethan sat up in his bed and looked around for the snake and edge of the cliff. But all he found was an old sock and the edge of his bed.

"I was dreaming!" Ethan said to himself with a smile. "That was a great dream!"

Ethan came down to the breakfast table carrying at least a dozen action figures. He had a bunch of dinosaurs, two aliens, a tank, a dump truck and, of course, Action Man, his favorite superhero.

Ethan put the figures around the table, under the napkin holder, and on top of the cereal box. He lined them up around his milk glass. He was getting ready for a huge fight between Action Man and the aliens. The dinosaurs were going to help out Action Man.

"Can you put those away while we have breakfast?" Ethan's mother asked. "The table is not a place for toys."

Ethan's mother sounded a little annoyed. She was sleepy, and she just wanted to have a quiet breakfast.

Then, as she was putting down a plate of scrambled eggs in front of Ethan, he grabbed one of the dinosaurs to chase away the aliens and spilled his milk all over the table and into his lap.

"Oh, Ethan," his mother said, "can't you be more careful? Now go upstairs and change your pants, and I'll clean up the table."

Ethan was out of his seat and he ran up the stairs in a flash. He tripped on the fourth stair and fell forward, but he was back up in a split second.

As he ran into his room, he could hear his mother say, "Are you all right, Ethan? Ethan? Ethan, answer me. Are you okay?"

Ethan didn't bother to answer his mother, because he knew that he was okay, and he would be downstairs soon.

Ethan should take his time and be more careful.

When Ethan got on the school bus, it was already filled with kids. He sat next to Freddy and across the aisle from Billy and Shawn, who were having a thumb-wrestling contest.

"I know that game," Ethan said, leaning almost out of his seat. He reached his arm across the aisle and started to grab Billy's thumb.

"Stop that, Ethan," Billy said. "Can't you see that we are already playing?"

"Cut it out," said Shawn. "Wait your turn."

But Ethan kept on trying to play. He thought it was fun to play with Billy and Shawn.

"What's going on back there?" said Mr. Banner, the school bus driver, looking in the mirror.

"Get back in your seat right now, Ethan, or you'll go straight to the principal's office when we get to school."

Ethan sat back in his seat, but he still kept looking at Billy and Shawn, who had turned away from Ethan, trying to ignore him. Ethan sat on his hands to try and keep them from reaching over and getting him into trouble again. That worked…but just barely. Fortunately, it was a short ride to school.

Ethan's morning went pretty much like all the other mornings in Mrs. Calhoun's class—constant trouble.

Mrs. Calhoun reminded Ethan to stay in his seat seven times.

Mrs. Calhoun moved Ethan to the front of the class, right in front of her desk, because he was bothering Mary Ellen while she worked.

Mrs. Calhoun told Ethan to stop sliding down in his seat, and to keep his hands off Patrick while they were lining up to go to the lunchroom, and to stop squirming while he was supposed to be doing silent reading.

Ethan didn't seem to mind being corrected over and over and over again, but Mrs. Calhoun didn't like it. No teacher likes correcting children all day long.

Mrs. Calhoun actually liked Ethan because he was smart and kind and funny, too. But she had to admit that he was a very difficult boy to teach.

That day at recess, Ethan was particularly wild and Mr. Kirby, the playground monitor, was concerned that Ethan might hurt himself.

Ethan climbed to the very top of the jungle gym and hung upside down. He leaned back on the swing so that his feet were entirely in the air and his head nearly brushed the ground. He joined a game of tag with some younger boys, but he hardly looked where he was going when he ran. He kept tripping them and knocking them over.

One boy, Aldo, fell and scraped his knee when Ethan tagged him too hard. Aldo cried very loudly, and his knee was full of blood. Ethan felt bad that Aldo was hurt, but there was nothing he could do to take it back. Mr. Kirby took Aldo to the nurse, and when he came back, he took Ethan to see the school principal.

Ethan sat in the principal's office for a long, long time. There was nothing to do. Ethan kept getting out of his seat, and the principal's secretary kept asking him to sit back down again.

While Ethan was waiting, his teacher, Mrs. Calhoun, walked in. She said, "Hello, Ethan," and went in to meet with the principal.

Then Ethan's mother came in. She said "Hello, Ethan," in a soft voice, and then she shook her head and went into the principal's office.

Next, Ethan's father came in. That wasn't good at all. Ethan's father said hello and smiled at him. Then he said, "This is serious business, son," and he went into the principal's office, too.

The principal's secretary said, "You can go back to your class, now, Ethan. Mrs. Calhoun will be there in a minute. Your parents will talk to you when you get home."

That night, Ethan had a family meeting with his mother and his father and his older brother, Nate. His father said that they were going to talk about Ethan's problem with self-control.

"What's self-control?" Ethan asked. "They didn't teach me that at school."

"That's exactly the problem," Ethan's father said. "It's not your fault that you are always getting into trouble. You just have too much energy, and no one has taught you how to control it."

"Self-control means slowing down when you need to, and sometimes even coming to a full stop. It's a little like driving a car. Sometimes you have to put on the gas, and sometimes you have to put on the brakes. You need to learn to use your brakes more often."

"Your teacher says that your school counselor, Mrs. Statler, helps children learn self-control, and we all agreed that you should see her every week."

The very next day, Ethan went to see Mrs. Statler.

Mrs. Statler shook Ethan's hand when she met him at the door. Then she said, "Have a seat anywhere you like, Ethan. We have lots to talk about today."

Ethan walked around Mrs. Statler's room, surprised to see all of the toys and games and dolls and puppets. He had never seen a room like this at school!

Within minutes, Ethan had dumped out a set of soldiers on the floor and started to play, forgetting that Mrs. Statler had asked him to take a seat.

But Mrs. Statler didn't seem upset that Ethan hadn't followed her request. She just got down on the floor with him and picked up one of the toy soldiers.

"I'm Captain Self-Control," Mrs. Statler said, pretending that it was the soldier talking and not her. "I'm going to teach you about different ways to control yourself so that you won't be getting into trouble all of the time. Okay, Private Ethan?"

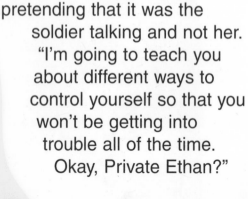

Ethan liked to play pretend soldiers. He played soldiers with his dad all of the time. He picked up one of the soldiers and said, "Okay, Captain! What do I do?"

"Well," said Mrs. Statler, in the voice of Captain Self-Control, "today we're going to put you on a Self-Control Point System. All of the soldiers in my squad go on a Self-Control Point System when they arrive, and that is how they earn the rank of Sergeant."

Mrs. Statler got up from the floor and went to her desk. She wrote on some paper for a few minutes while Ethan lined up some of the soldiers. Then she came back to the floor.

Mrs. Statler gave Ethan a sheet of paper.

"This is your Point Chart," she said, still pretending to be Captain Self-Control. There are five things you must do to earn points:

1. Do what adults ask of you right away.
2. Finish your work and check it over to make sure it is right.
3. Wait your turn to talk or when playing with other children.
4. Keep your things organized.
5. Don't rush through things.

"When you do each of these things, you will get one point from your mom and one point from your teacher. If you try hard really hard, you can get ten points for the whole day. But if you misbehave and break an important rule, you will lose a point."

"Then we'll add up all of the points that you earned each day. If you can earn 30 points in one week—that's less than five points a day—you will get to pick a prize from my Treasure Chest. When you do this for a whole month, you can be a sergeant in the Self-Control Squad."

Daily Point Chart

Day _____ Date _____

Rules	Home	School
		(enter a "+" or "-" sign)
Do what adults ask	☐	☐
Finish your work and check it over	☐	☐
Wait your turn to talk or when playing with other children	☐	☐
Keep your things organized	☐	☐
Don't rush through things	☐	☐
Daily Total:	☐	☐

The next day was Saturday and Ethan couldn't wait to start his Self-Control Point Chart. He really wanted to get a prize from Mrs. Statler's Treasure Chest.

Mrs. Statler had called Ethan's mother, and she knew all about the chart. Mrs. Statler had also given her a list of things that she could do around the house, which would help Ethan earn enough points to get a prize and be in the Self-Control Squad.

Ethan's mother organized his toys so that it would be easier for him to put them away.

She organized his desk so that he would have the supplies he needed to do his homework and so that he wouldn't lose his work when it was done.

Ethan's mother got him a timer so that he would know how long to work. Ethan was supposed to work for 15 minutes at a time.

Ethan's mother also made a daily "To Do" list for Ethan that showed all of the things he had to do. Ethan checked off each one after he did it.

To Do List:

1. Straighten up your room

2. Finish your homework

3. Read a chapter in your book

4. Have fun!

Mrs. Statler also said that Ethan would do better when he got a "cue"—a reminder that he was supposed to slow down and focus on what he was doing. Ethan's mother held up one finger and waved it side to side, as a secret sign for Ethan to help him slow down and put on the brakes.

At the end of the day, Ethan earned three points. He earned another two points on Sunday.

On Monday, Ethan brought his Self-Control Point Chart to school in his newly organized backpack. His homework was in a special folder with Action Man on the front, and his pencils and pens were in a purple plastic case.

Ethan handed his chart to Mrs. Calhoun, and she took it with a smile.

"I talked to Mrs. Statler," she said, "and I think that your Point Chart is a good idea. I'll go over it with you after school every day, and we'll send it home to your mom."

"Mrs. Statler also gave me some other ideas to help you stay focused on your assignments. She said that you will do better on your assignments if they are more active. I think that all of the kids will like that, too. She suggested that you could have a buddy to check your assignments when they are complete, and I think that is a good idea for everyone, too. Your buddy will be Shawn."

"I'm also going to have a secret signal to give you when I see that you need to focus and pay attention to the rules on your chart. I'm going to scratch my head, just above my ear, and that will mean that you are getting close to losing a point. No one will know this signal except you and me."

"Mrs. Statler also said to give you plenty of praise when you do well, and I know that is going to be easy to do!"

Ethan tried very hard all day long at school to earn points. He had his own copy of the things he had to do on his Self-Control Point Chart, and he thought he did them all pretty well.

Of course, Ethan wasn't perfect. It's hard to learn new habits, and no one is perfect at first.

At the end of the day, Ethan saw that he got two points taken away. Mrs. Calhoun said that this was for talking when he was supposed to be working and running down the hall instead of walking.

She also said how proud she was of Ethan, and that she saw a big improvement in his self-control already.

"You earned two points at school today," Mrs. Calhoun said. "I'm sure that you can earn more points at home, too."

When it was Friday, it was time to see Mrs. Statler again.

He sat at the breakfast table and although he was very excited, Ethan stayed in his seat.

There were no toys on the breakfast table any more. His mother had said that he would lose a point if he played at the table, and Ethan didn't intend to lose any points if he could help it!

But he did have his Self-Control Point Chart next to him. His mother said that was okay.

Ethan was very proud of his charts. He had earned a total of 33 points. That was more than enough points to earn a prize from the Treasure Chest. Ethan wondered about what he would get. Maybe a special soldier? Maybe a dinosaur? Maybe a rubber bug he had seen in the Treasure Chest the first time he visited Mrs. Statler?

Whatever he chose, he knew there would be some great fun ahead.

Here are some of the things that Ethan learned about self-control.

- It is important to calm down and concentrate at certain times of the day, like when you are eating a meal at home, or when you are doing work at school.

- It is important to keep your things organized.

- It is important to complete your work, and to check and make sure that it is correct.

- When you learn self-control you get into trouble less often, and your parents and teachers are proud of you.

- Sometimes kids need help learning self-control. A point system will help you keep track of your progress and you can win prizes, too!

Teaching Children Self-Control

There are different theories as to why some children have a hard time learning self-control and others do not, but everyone agrees that learning self-control is an important part of a child's emotional development. Children with good self-control not only do better in school, but they also tend to have more friends, and more self-confidence.

A point system, like the one described in this book, is usually the first technique used to help children develop better self-control. There are many other things you can do as well, like setting clear rules and limits, cutting down on the things that distract children from their work, and of course setting a good example with your own behavior.

Many children that have ongoing problems in self-control are diagnosed as having ADHD or other behavioral problems. These children need special consideration, and there are many professionals who can help. A complete evaluation is always needed to understand the reasons for the problem. Changes typically need to be made in the home as well as the classroom, and these should be included in a comprehensive treatment plan. Sometimes medication will be prescribed, but while medication can help, it does not teach children self-control. Only caring adults and patient adults can do that.

Other Great Books from
the Emotional Literacy Series

To place an order or to get a catalog,
please write, call, or visit our web-site.

CTC Publishing
A Division of Courage To Change
10400 Eaton Place, Suite 140
Fairfax, Virginia 22030
1-800-942-0962
www.couragetochange.com

The Emotional Literacy Series

- Hardcover library bindings
- More than 40 pages each, full-color illustrations throughout
- Reading level: Grade 2

This new book series helps children understand their emotions and behaviors with friendly advice from Dr. Larry and a gang of amusing cartoon characters. Each book explores a particular topic — anger, teasing, excess energy, childhood obesity and peer pressure — from the point of view of the child, and offers child-friendly advice on how to deal with the problem. Each book begins with a letter to the boys and girls reading the book from the author, Dr. Larry Shapiro. Dr. Larry introduces the subject in a reassuring, non-judgmental tone and tells kids: "All feelings are okay. It's what you do with them that counts!"

Arnold Gets Angry

Everyone gets angry sometimes. In this appealing book, Arnold and his friends learn about what makes them angry...and how to control their anger by talking about it to friends, parents, teachers. The book is child-friendly and fun to read as it teaches problem-solving skills that really work! ISBN: 0-9747789-0-7

67312   Arnold Gets Angry...................................**$17.95**

Betty Stops the Bully

Nobody likes to be bullied or teased. And many children, like Betty, don't know how to make it stop. This story suggests sensible things to do when confronted by a bully. It also helps children who are bullies learn new social skills. ISBN: 0-9747789-1-5

67313   Betty Stops the Bully........................$17.95

Catherine Finds Her Courage

All kids are scared sometimes. Fear is a normal part of life. But some children have fears that impede their learning and making friends. This book helps children recognize some of the most common fears of childhood. ISBN: 0-9747789-2-3

67314   Catherine Finds Her Courage $17.95

Freddie Fights Fat

Being overweight is a problem for a lot of kids. Freddy didn't think he was chubby, until he noticed his clothes were too tight and he couldn't keep up with the other kids in sports. This story teaches children how to change bad eating habits and lose weight by eating healthier foods, exercising, and spending less time in front of the TV. ISBN: 0-9747789-5-8

67873   Freddie Fights Fat $17.95

Debra Doesn't Take The Dare

Peer pressure is a challenge for anyone. This story follows Debra as she faces peer pressure when dared to drink a beer as part of the initiation to a cool girl's club. Children learn to question what is right for them and to seek the advice of adults. The story offers children helpful suggestions for coping with peer pressure and standing up for what is right for them, or more importantly, what is not.

(Ages 4 to 12.) ISBN: 0-9747789-3-1

20705   Soft Cover, 54 pages..$17.95

Also from CTC Publishing...

Games (and more) to Keep Families Connected

We know that the time parents and children spend together is special – a chance to share experiences, create memories and learn about one another. So, we are creating a series of games (and more) that help families learn new ways to communicate and have fun together, too. There are games designed for dads and kids – and moms, too. There are even games and postcard sets available for parents who are apart from their children. Playing these games takes very little time, and it helps develop a closer relationship between parents and children as they act out activities and get a chance to talk about feelings in a playful, non-threatening way.

Hey, Dad — Let's Talk
For 2-5 players. Ages 3+

Because fathers sometimes find it hard to talk to their kids...and kids sometimes find it hard to talk to their dads...

We've created *Hey, Dad — Let's Talk,* an exciting new board game to help dads and kids learn new ways to communicate and have fun together, too!

Hey, Dad — Let's Talk is easy and fun to play; kids as young as three can enjoy it! And it's a game in which *everyone wins and nobody loses.*

The players take turns rolling the dice and moving their game pieces around the board. Along the way, players must follow the instructions on the board or pick a card from one of the three decks.

Fun Factory cards are activity oriented; the player may have to tell a joke while standing on one foot. *Talking Cards* may ask the player to describe his or her favorite dinner. *Memory Makers* cards may ask the player to give a compliment to another player. Special cards for preschool-aged children are also included.

When all the players have circled the board, everyone joins hands and shares in the prize.

67779   *Hey, Dad — Let's Talk* Game...$29.95

Would you like to learn more about how this wonderful game can be used as the focus of a Playful Parenting Night? And get some tips on how to hold a workshop for parents and how to fund it? Please call Dede Pitts, VP, at: 1-800-942-0962 or e-mail her at: pitts@ndmc.com."

Coming Soon: *Hey, Mom – Let's Talk*

Hey, Dad — Let's Learn!
Early Learning Activity Cards

Designed to strengthen the ties between fathers and their young children, the ninety cards in this deck provide ninety imaginative learning activities that take just a few minutes each to do.

Dads and their kids make music with rubber bands, do silly dances, take nature walks, make shaving-cream mustaches, look for circles around the house, and more. The activities are both simple and fun, and they make dads into great teachers, with a focus on basic preschool concepts such as colors, shapes, letter recognition, putting things in a sequence, and talking about feelings.

68018   *Hey Dad, Let's Learn!* $15.95

Hi, Dad, Let's Write!
A postcard set for dads and kids

These cards were designed to help dads play an important role in their children's lives even though they may be far apart. (Moms can use them too!) The set contains two packs of 25 postcards, one for dads to send to their kids and one for kids to send to their dads.

Each postcard is preprinted with a "thought starter" to help the writer get started: *"I'll tell you something funny that happened ..."* or *"If you were here right now we'd ..."* or *"You won't believe what happened in school today ..."*, for example.

When it's not possible for fathers to be with their children, sending frequent messages openly expressing thoughts and feelings can make a tremendous difference in developing a positive relationship.

68070   Hi Dad — Let's Write postcard set $17.95